WHERE IS THE STAR?

To my (not-so-little) stars—Kaitlin,
William, Matthew, Joshua, and Nathan.

May you always shine bright.

—S.H.

ISBN 13: 978-1-4621-3754-1

Published by CFI, an imprint of Cedar Fort, Inc.
2373 W. 700 S., Springville, UT 84663
Distributed by Cedar Fort, Inc., www.cedarfort.com

Library of Congress Control Number: 2020945605

Cover design and typesetting by Shawnda T. Craig
Cover design © 2020 Cedar Fort, Inc.

Printed in the United States of America

10 9 8 7 6 5 4 3 2 1

Printed on acid-free paper

WHERE IS THE STAR?

WRITTEN BY: STEFANIE HOHL

ILLUSTRATED BY: JEFIMIJA

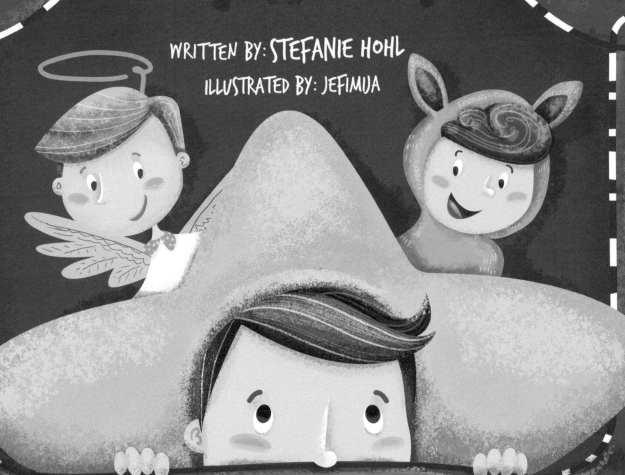

CFI · AN IMPRINT OF CEDAR FORT, INC. · SPRINGVILLE, UTAH

There are the children,
dressing with glee.

There are the buildings,
painted and set.

There are the people,
waiting to see.

But where, oh where,
is the STAR?

There is sweet Mary, heavy with child.
There is kind Joseph, leading the way.

There is the donkey,
ever so mild.

But where, oh where,
is the STAR?

There is the innkeeper, telling them no.
There is the stable, cozy and dry.

There is a lantern, soft light aglow.
But where, oh where, is the STAR?

There are the cattle, mooing with pride.
There are the chickens, clucking so soft.

There are the field mice, huddled inside.
But where, oh where, is the STAR?

There is the manger,
bursting with hay.

There is the mother,
beaming with love.

There is the baby, born on that day.
But where, oh where, is the STAR?

There are the angels,
singing their joy.

There are the grazers,
woolly heads low.

There are the shepherds, praising the boy.

But where, oh where, is the STAR?

There are the camels,
thirsty and bold.

There are the wise men,
in from the East.

There is the incense, gifts made of gold.

But where, oh where, is the STAR?

There it is twinkling, high above Earth,
Announcing to all the Christ Child's birth.